Celia Warren

Illustrated by Mike Terry

Walrus lived on the cold ice at the North Pole.

One day Walrus said, "I would love to go and see my friend, Penguin."

So Walrus left his home and set off on the long journey to the South Pole.

Penguin lived on the cold ice at the South Pole.

On the very same day Penguin said, "I would love to go and see my friend, Walrus."

So Penguin left her home and set off on the long journey to the North Pole.

Walrus had not gone far when he met some huskies. They took him for a ride in a sleigh. Walrus was so excited that he sent a postcard to Penguin.

Dear Penguin,
I am on my way to visit you.
Today I went for a ride in a sleigh.
I can't wait to see you.
Your friend,
Walrus

Penguin,
South Pole

Meanwhile, Penguin was in Australia. She met some friendly kangaroos. They showed her how to jump. Penguin was so excited that she sent a postcard to Walrus.

AUSTRALIA
Dear Walrus,
I am on my way to visit you.
I am having fun jumping with the kangaroos.
I will see you soon.
Your friend,
Penguin
Walrus,
North Pole

Meanwhile, Walrus swam and swam until he came to Hawaii. He met some people on the beach. They put a garland of flowers around his neck and showed him how to dance.

Walrus couldn't wait to tell Penguin, so he sent her a postcard.

Meanwhile, Penguin traveled on. She came to China. She saw a wonderful firework display and a dancing dragon. Penguin sent Walrus a postcard.

Dear Walrus,
I can't wait to tell you about the wonderful fireworks and the dancing dragon.
I will see you soon.
Your friend,
Penguin

Walrus,
North Pole

Walrus came to a rain forest in Brazil, where he met a parrot.

"I am too hot," said Walrus.

"I am too hot," said the parrot.

"I miss my nice ice," said Walrus.

"I miss my nice ice," said the parrot.

"Good-bye," said Walrus.

"Good-bye," said the parrot.

Walrus sent a postcard to Penguin.

BRAZIL
Dear Penguin,
I am in a hot rain forest
with a talking parrot.
I wish you were here!
I miss my nice ice and
I can't wait to see you.
Your friend,
Walrus
Penguin,
South Pole

Walrus and Penguin traveled over

land and sea until they came to Egypt.

Walrus went to look at the pyramids. Penguin went to look at the pyramids. Then they met!

"Walrus, it's you!" laughed Penguin.

"Penguin, it's you!" laughed Walrus. They were so happy to see one another.

Then they had some adventures together.
They had a ride on a train–
a camel train!

They visited a museum.
Walrus learned another dance.